The
Very Ordinary
Caterpillar

Written and Illustrated by
Garry Fleming

WELDON
KiDS

Once there was a caterpillar,

a Very Ordinary Caterpillar.

He looked up one day and saw
that the sky was endlessly blue.

And all around him
flowers bloomed
in so many colours
he could not
count them.

Two beautifully coloured Rainbow Lorikeets
flew over, and landed beside him.
'Why do you have so many beautiful colours, and I do not?'
asked the Very Ordinary Caterpillar.

'Because we are
Rainbow Lorikeets,'
they laughed.

'And you are just a
Very Ordinary Caterpillar.'

Below on the forest floor, a bird with feathers
that shimmered like satin was strutting about.
'Why do you have feathers that shine like satin, and I do not?'
asked the Very Ordinary Caterpillar.

'Because I am a Satin Bowerbird,'
he said, bowing proudly.
'And you are just a
Very Ordinary Caterpillar.'

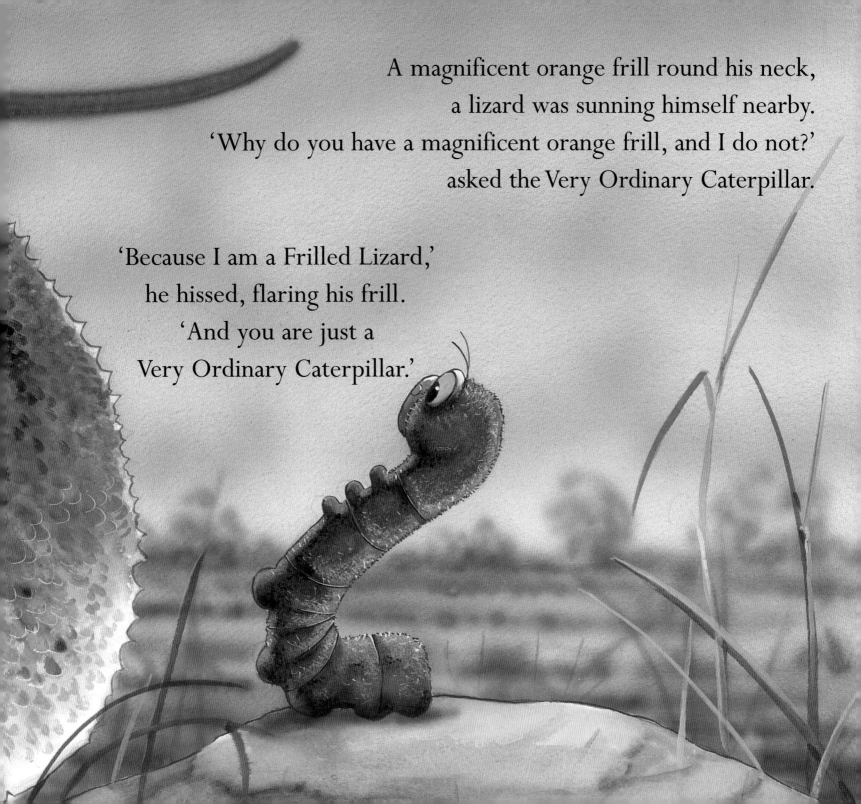

A magnificent orange frill round his neck,
a lizard was sunning himself nearby.
'Why do you have a magnificent orange frill, and I do not?'
asked the Very Ordinary Caterpillar.

'Because I am a Frilled Lizard,'
he hissed, flaring his frill.
'And you are just a
Very Ordinary Caterpillar.'

Just then a big green frog with bright red eyes,
came hopping past the Very Ordinary Caterpillar.
'Why do you have bright red eyes and I do not?'
asked the Very Ordinary Caterpillar.

'Because I am a Red-eyed Frog,'
he croaked.
'And you are just a
Very Ordinary Caterpillar.'

Creeping out from between the leaves
came an orange creature with big white spots.
'Why do you have so many big white spots,
and I do not?'
asked the Very Ordinary Caterpillar.

'Because I am a Spotted Cuscus,'
he said oh so slowly.
'And you are just a
Very Ordinary Caterpillar.'

'I don't have shiny feathers
or a magnificent orange frill,
I don't have red eyes,
spots or rainbow colours,

'I really am a Very Ordinary Caterpillar,'
Said the Very Ordinary Caterpillar.
and with that he spun himself a cocoon to hide.

And that's where he stayed,
till one day…

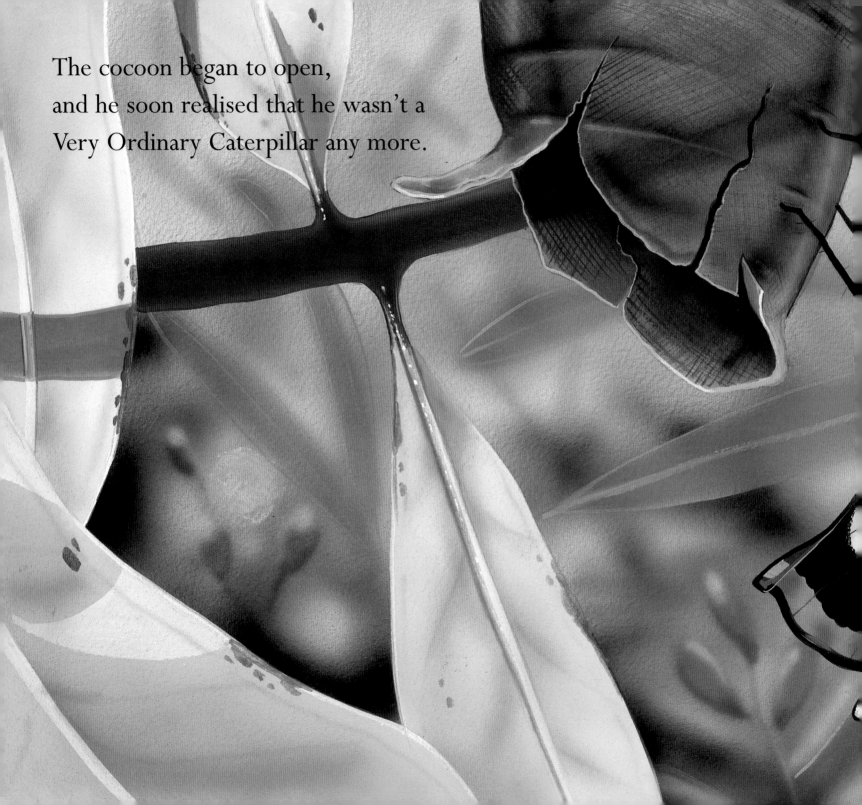

The cocoon began to open,
and he soon realised that he wasn't a
Very Ordinary Caterpillar any more.

His wings shimmered like satin,
with more colours than a rainbow.
They were edged in orange frill
and covered in white spots,
and right in the middle of both
wings were two bright circles
that looked just like eyes.

The Very Ordinary Caterpillar was now a very Extraordinary Butterfly.